FRANKIE VS. THE ROWDY ROMANS

ALSO BY FRANK LAMPARD

FRANKIE VS. THE ROWDY ROMANS

FRANK LAMPARD

SCHOLASTIC INC.

ISBN 978-0-545-66614-5

Published by Scholastic Inc., 557 Broadway, New York, NY 10012, by arrangement with Little, Brown Books for Young Readers. SCHOLASTIC and associated logos are trademarks and/or registered trademarks of Scholastic Inc.

12 11 10 9 8 7 6 5 4 3 2   14 15 16 17 18 19/0

Printed in the U.S.A.   40
First printing, June 2014

To my mom, Pat,
who encouraged me to do my
homework in between kicking a ball
all around the house, and is still
with me every step of the way

*Welcome to a fantastic
fantasy league — the greatest
soccer competition ever held in
this world or any other!*

*You'll need four on a team,
so choose carefully. This is a lot
more serious than a game in the
park. You'll never know who your
next opponents will be, or where
you'll face them.*

*So lace up your cleats, players,
and good luck! The whistle's
about to blow!*

The Ref

CHAPTER 1

Frankie pushed the bell beside Charlie's front door.

DING-DONG!

"It must have been a dream," said Louise, who was standing next to him.

"But we all had the *same* dream," said Frankie.

Louise rolled her eyes. "There's no such thing as a magic soccer ball," she said. "And even if there were, it wouldn't look like that." She pointed to the ball under Frankie's arm.

He smiled. The ball looked like it had been chewed up and spit out. Half the leather had peeled away, and it sagged like an old balloon. He'd won it at a carnival from a strange old man, but something very weird had happened when they had played with the ball in the park. A portal into another world had opened up, and they'd found themselves on a wooden ship, playing soccer against pirates. Well, three pirates and a talking parrot, which was even weirder.

"We can't have been dreaming," said Frankie. "It was the middle of the day."

He heard the sound of footsteps in the house. Max, Frankie's dog, barked.

"And dogs don't talk, either," said Louise.

Max glanced up. On the pirate ship, he'd been chatting away like one of them. But back in the real world, it was just his usual barks, whines, and growls.

The door opened and Charlie stood there. He was wearing his goalie gloves, as always, and was holding a slice of toast.

"Sorry, guys, just finishing my breakfast," he said.

Louise laughed. "It might be easier if you took those off," she said, nodding at the gloves.

Charlie shook his head. "No way. The best goalies are —"

"— always ready!" said Louise and Frankie together. They had heard it a million times.

Charlie swallowed the last bit of toast. "Let's go."

Just as he stepped through the

door, his kitten, Jinx, slipped out after him. Max leapt into the air, then scurried away, tail between his legs. Jinx purred and narrowed her green eyes.

"She's nothing to be frightened of," said Frankie, scratching Max behind the ears.

Jinx leapt up onto the front fence and arched her back.

"She's just a pussycat," said Louise, running her hand over Jinx's fur.

As the friends set off toward the park, Max seemed to recover, trotting a few steps ahead of them and sniffing around.

"It's funny how your dog is so fearless about everything else," said Charlie, "but he's terrified of Jinx."

Frankie shrugged. "I guess we're all scared of something. It doesn't have to make sense. I don't like heights."

"I *hate* spiders," said Louise.

They were silent for a few seconds, then Louise asked, "What are you scared of, Charlie?"

"I don't know," said Charlie, chewing his lip. "Nothing, I guess. No, actually, I do know! I'm scared of . . . not saving goals."

Frankie and Louise burst out laughing.

"That doesn't count!" said Frankie.

"Well, I suppose I'm scared of sharks," said Charlie.

"We're *all* scared of sharks," said Frankie. He shuddered as he remembered seeing shark fins cutting through the waves beside the pirate ship. "Do you think it was real?" he asked.

Charlie shrugged. "It felt real to me. Has anything else happened with the ball since?"

Frankie shook his head. "Nope." He'd tried playing with it in his backyard and even in his bedroom. No more portals had opened up.

It was sort of a relief—on the pirate ship, they'd almost ended up marooned on a desert island. But Frankie couldn't help feeling disappointed, too. "I've got a theory, though," he said. "Maybe it only works when we're all together."

"Frankie's FC might not be finished yet!" said Louise.

A light drizzle had started by the time they reached the park, so there weren't many people around. Frankie dropped his ball and kicked it into Charlie's gloves.

"Looks like we'll get the field to ourselves," said Charlie as they made their way to the grass where they played.

"Or not," said Louise, pointing ahead. "Uh-oh."

Frankie looked up and his heart sank. His older brother, Kevin, was already there with his friends Liam, Rob, and Matt. Matt was in goal between the two posts. They were kicking around a brand-new soccer ball.

"Whoa!" said Charlie. "That's a 'Pro Infinity.' They cost a lot."

Frankie felt himself blushing. He suddenly wanted to hide his battered old ball. "Come on, let's go somewhere else."

But it was too late. His brother blasted a shot past Matt and the ball rolled toward Frankie. He stopped it under his foot.

"Look who it is!" said Kevin. "*Frankenstein* and his loser friends."

Frankie's embarrassment turned to anger. He put up with his brother picking on him, but not his friends. *Time to teach them a lesson*, he thought. "Hi, Kev," he said. "Can we play, too?"

Kevin glanced at his friends as he walked over. "No way," he sneered. "It's not a *children's* game."

Kevin tried to kick the ball from under Frankie's foot, but Frankie rolled it back out of reach.

"Give me the ball, Frankenstein," said Kevin, his face darkening. "Or else."

"Sure," said Frankie. He dribbled

the ball over to his brother, then tipped it through his legs.

"Hey!" said Kevin. "I said, give —"

Frankie wasn't listening. He passed the ball to Louise. Liam and Rob were closing in. Louise faked a pass back to Frankie but took the ball around Rob. Charlie was laughing. "Go, Frankie's team!" he shouted. Liam was a big kid, and he was quick. He ran at Louise, but she kept steady and flicked the ball over his head. It came to Frankie, who was now in front of the goal.

Matt spread his arms. "You're not getting past me," he said.

Want to bet? thought Frankie.

"Hey, that's ours!" came Charlie's voice.

Frankie turned, forgetting about shooting. Max was barking, running in circles around Kevin, who was holding their soccer ball from the carnival.

"*Children* play in the *children's* area," Kevin said. "Now, beat it!" He tossed the old ball in the air, then booted it high and far.

Frankie watched his ball fly toward the toddlers' play area.

Suddenly, he was on the ground, as Liam tackled him roughly and took the other ball.

"Great shot, Kev!" called Matt. He lowered his voice and muttered to Frankie, "Told you that you wouldn't score."

CHAPTER 2

Frankie picked himself up, hanging his head and avoiding his brother's look as he joined his friends. Together, they trudged off to find their ball.

"Just ignore him," said Louise. "Your brother's only jealous because you're better at soccer than he is."

"Yeah," said Charlie, grinning.

"He's probably jealous of your ball, too."

Frankie looked at his friend, who was smirking. He couldn't help smiling, too. His ball had cost him fifty cents rather than fifty dollars.

The rain began to fall much harder. Great gray sheets poured from the sky, so it was hard to see very far ahead. Behind them, Frankie could hear Kevin and his friends shouting that they should find some shelter.

"We'd better go, too," said Frankie. This was turning into a disaster. "Max, go and get the ball."

Max streaked off. Frankie squinted ahead and saw his dog pause for a moment on the edge of the playground. Then he darted toward the sandbox, and leapt over the side.

He vanished with a howl.

"Max!" called Frankie.

"What happened to him?" said Louise, panic in her voice.

Frankie broke into a run. He was soaked to the skin now. He hopped over the fence into the play area and ran to the sandbox's edge.

The sand was gone, replaced by a pool of swirling colors.

"It's just like the portal from

before," said Charlie, huffing as he caught up.

Frankie nodded slowly. "Max must have fallen through," he mumbled.

"What should we do?" asked Charlie.

Frankie stared into his friends' faces. Rain had matted their hair and soaked their clothes. "I can't ask you to come with me," he said. "Max is my dog. He's my responsibility."

"We're coming," said Louise. "No question. The best teams always stick together."

"She's right," said Charlie. "Try stopping us."

Frankie's heart surged with relief. *I never should have doubted them.*

He held out both hands, and Louise and Charlie each took one. Whatever waited for them on the other side, they'd face it together. "Ready?" he asked.

Charlie gave a quick nod and Louise squeezed his hand tighter.

Frankie leapt into the kaleidoscope of color. Both of his friends' hands were wrenched from his. Everything went dark.

The first thing Frankie realized was that he was dry. Dry and warm.

That's a good start, he thought.

"Louise?" he said. "Charlie?"

"I can't see anything," said Louise.

"Me, neither," whimpered Charlie. "And, by the way, I *am* afraid of something — the dark!"

"Don't worry," said Frankie, groping about in the gloom. Metal clanked and the sound echoed. Frankie shuffled forward. More clanking, and he almost tripped.

"I've got chains around my ankles," he said.

The sound of shifting chains seemed to come from all around him.

"Me too," said Louise.

"Oh, great!" said Charlie.

A low growl rumbled in the air.

"Jinx?" said Charlie.

"That sounded *bigger* than Jinx," said a husky voice that Frankie recognized.

"Is that you, Max?" he said. He felt a wet nose brush his leg.

"Sorry I got you all into this mess," said Max.

"What mess?" said Charlie. "Where *are* we?"

Frankie suddenly heard whistling, and a faint glow appeared in the distance. It grew brighter, until he saw it was the flickering flame of a torch in the hand of a large man. He also made out thick wooden stakes and iron bars all around them.

"We're in a cage!" he said.

The man holding the torch walked toward one side of the cage. With him came a breeze of smelly air: old feet and rotten onions. Judging by the man's toothless, dirt- and sweat-smeared face, Frankie guessed he was the source of the smell. He looked a bit like Frankie's next-door neighbor, Mr. Pratchett – if Mr. Pratchett hadn't been to the dentist in about a hundred years.

"Hey!" said Charlie, rushing to the bars as fast as his chains would allow. "Let us out of here!"

The man scowled, and another wave of stinkiness almost knocked Frankie off his feet.

"Oh, you'll be out of there soon enough," he said. "Your team's up next."

"Our team?" said Frankie. He looked down and realized he was wearing a dirty white tunic and leather sandals. On his chest was the same badge that had appeared when he had faced the pirates. It read *FFC*.

"Frankie's Football Club," he said to himself. "Guys, we're going to play another match!"

"Hurray!" said Louise. She was wearing a tattered tunic, too, with a cape behind it.

"Let's hope we're not getting fed to the sharks at the end," said Charlie.

Their jailer frowned. "No sharks today," he hissed. "They're not flooding the arena until next week."

Arena? thought Frankie. *Where are we?* He knew someone who could tell him. "Can we speak to the Ref?" he asked.

The jailer bashed the cage bars with his torch. "Who's this 'Ref'?" he snarled. "One of the other gladiators?"

"Gladiators?" said Louise. She gripped Frankie's shoulder. "We must be in ancient Rome!"

The jailer shook his head. "You're a funny bunch, aren't you? We just call it Rome."

An enormous roar shook Frankie to his bones.

"That sounded *a lot* bigger than Jinx," said Max.

The jailer smiled. "That's Ferox. Better pray he's not hungry. Ha! What am I saying? Ferox is *always* hungry."

Charlie's eyes were as big as saucers.

"You ready?" said the jailer, opening the door of the cage.

"No!" yelled Frankie and his friends.

CHAPTER 3

The jailer led them along a low corridor. They shuffled and rattled along in their chains. Torchlight threw long shadows on the walls. Every few steps, they passed alcoves that led to other cells. In the gloom, Frankie made out figures crouched in their cages: just whites of eyes, with the occasional glint of steel armor and swords. The air smelled of stale sweat and fear.

They must be the other gladiators, he thought. *They don't look much like soccer players!*

From somewhere above came the hum of voices: hundreds, maybe thousands of them. Frankie felt a bead of sweat trickle down his cheek. His heart was thumping in his chest.

The jailer led them around several corners, and then up a long ramp toward a towering wooden gate.

"Perhaps we should go back to that nice warm cage," muttered Max.

The jailer raised his torch and banged three times on the wooden gate. He turned to Frankie and his friends. "Too late for that now," he said. "Your audience awaits!"

A rhythmic thumping began on the other side of the gate. Frankie realized that the crowd was stamping their feet in unison.

As the jailer walked between them, unlocking the chains at their ankles, the pounding grew louder, and faster and faster, until it felt as if the walls were shaking.

"We'll be all right," Frankie said to the others.

The jailer grinned. "They all say that."

The hinges groaned as the gates swung outward.

Frankie was blinded and deafened at once. Daylight flooded the rampway, and the roar of voices created a wall of sound. He rocked back on his heels, but the jailer gave him a shove in the back.

"Wow!" said Louise.

Frankie stumbled through the gates. Blinking into the glare, he gasped. Steep tiers of seats rose up on every side of the arena, with great stone arches built one on top of the other. The stands were packed with what must have been thirty thousand people, all wearing tunics or togas of every color, or dresses draped in many folds. Their eyes stared at him. Frankie turned slowly. He and his friends were standing on one side of an enormous circular field, but instead of grass on the ground, there was a thin layer of sand over hard-packed earth. He felt tiny, as if he were waiting on a long line at a fair.

"This is the Colosseum!" said Louise. "We learned about it at school. It's one of the largest buildings in ancient Rome, built in the first century for gladiatorial contests . . ."

"Not soccer matches?" said Charlie.

"No," said Frankie with a giant gulp. "Fights to the death."

"Oh," said Max. "And I was just hoping for a run in the park."

From somewhere in the arena, a drum beat slowly. Two servants with bare chests began to close the gates behind them, and the jailer gave them a little wave.

"See you soon!" called Charlie bravely.

"I doubt it," said the jailer. Then

the gates slammed closed and he was gone.

The drums sped up, hammering more quickly. Frankie noticed that the eyes of the crowd had all shifted in one direction. He followed them with his own and saw a man standing far from them across the arena. He wore black and had some sort of necklace hanging around his neck. "Guys!" Frankie said. "Look!"

The black-clad man made his way to a raised podium as the drumbeat quickened to a crescendo. As he lowered himself into a throne-like seat, the drums stopped dead.

"That's not right," said Louise, frowning. "That's where the emperor should sit. But he wore purple, not black."

Frankie suddenly realized what the necklace was — a whistle. And now he recognized the face, too. "It's not the emperor," he said. "It's the Ref!"

"Welcome, challengers!" bellowed a bald man beside the Ref. "State your team name!"

Frankie cleared his throat. He wasn't going to let his fear get the better of him. "Frankie's FC!" he called.

Thousands of boos rolled in

from the stands. The noise was incredible — shouts and screams and hisses.

"We're definitely the away team," said Louise nervously.

The Ref reached down and picked up something round off of a stand in front of him. He lifted it above his head.

"The ball!" said Frankie. "*Our* ball!"

The Ref hurled the ball into the arena. It rolled to a stop right in the center.

"Where's the goal?" Charlie shouted.

Two pairs of servants appeared at opposite sides of the field. They lifted two pairs of posts into position, facing each other.

"This should be easy," said Max, scampering toward the ball. "The other side hasn't even shown up!" Suddenly a trumpet blared, and Max froze.

"Welcome the Rowdy Romans!" cried the bald announcer at the Ref's side.

The gates opposite Frankie and his team burst open in a cloud of sand and dust, and two figures entered. They couldn't have looked more different. One was a skinny, bare-chested man who must have weighed about the same as Frankie.

He wore a helmet, a studded belt, and a kind of leather skirt. Clutching a long, pronged trident in one hand, he dragged a net in the other.

Next to him stood a giant: a man over seven feet tall. His helmet was big and shiny on his head, while his chest and arms were clad in thick, dented armor. He carried a heavy club.

"Beware Snatcher and Brutus!" yelled the announcer. The crowd cheered. "And their leader..." he continued, "Captain Lasher!"

The cries became wilder as a horse charged into the arena, scattering

the servants who'd opened the gates. The horse pulled a chariot in which stood a tall woman wearing tight-fitting leather armor and cracking a whip in the air. At the center of the arena, she pulled back sharply on the reins, and the chariot skidded to a halt. Behind it, the dust settled.

Captain Lasher turned her steely gaze on Frankie and his team and smiled. "This shouldn't take long," she said.

CHAPTER 4

"We're toast," said Charlie. "Even if we *do* have one more player than they do."

"They're not that scary," said Louise, throwing a glance toward Brutus. "Remember when we played Kennedy Elementary? They had a big defender, too."

He didn't have a club, though, thought Frankie.

The Ref blew his whistle and the announcer turned over a large hourglass filled with sand. "Let the battle commence!"

Frankie and his teammates ran for the ball. At the same time, Captain Lasher sent her horse forward with a whipcrack. She also appeared to be holding something at waist level with her other hand, while balancing perfectly in the chariot.

What's she up to? Frankie wondered.

THWANG!

Frankie saw something spinning by the side of her chariot, and realized too late what it was. A *slingshot!*

A ball of wood the size of his head hurtled toward him. Just before it hit, a shape leapt to his side. Charlie caught the ball in his gloves and it thumped into the sand.

"Thanks!" said Frankie.

THWANG!

Another ball shot out, this time heading straight for Max. The little dog froze.

Charlie dove across to stop the shot, catching it in midair.

"Great save," called Max. "I was almost a fur pancake!"

"That's a foul!" cried Louise.

Captain Lasher drew her chariot alongside the ball and scooped it up in one hand.

"*And* that!" said Louise. "Handball!"

Frankie looked up hopefully at the Ref, but he was sitting now, hardly paying attention: One servant was fanning him with a huge plume of peacock feathers; another was offering him a goblet and a platter of grapes.

Captain Lasher cackled. "Silly girl! There aren't any rules in the

Colosseum!" She tugged hard on the reins and began steering her chariot toward the goal.

Frankie knew he couldn't catch up to a galloping horse. His eyes landed on one of the wooden balls. Without stopping to think, he grabbed it, spun around, and hurled it with a grunt. *If I can just distract her . . .*

The wooden ball landed right in the chariot's path. Captain Lasher pulled hard at the reins to avoid it, and the chariot tipped as one wheel left the ground. "Aaah!" she cried, as it toppled sideways.

Frankie winced as she spilled out

onto the dust. The soccer ball rolled loose and Louise was quickly on it.

Captain Lasher climbed to her feet and began to right her fallen chariot. Frankie was glad she wasn't hurt. "You won't get away with this!" she yelled.

But the crash had broken her slingshot. *Now to win the game.* "Louise! Go!" Frankie shouted, pointing to the goal. His friend turned and began to run. But Brutus was now lumbering into her path.

"On the wing!" called Max. "Pass it! Pass it!"

Louise looked up, saw Max, and went to pass. But then a net landed silently over her head, and tangled up her feet. She fell headlong in a heap.

"Gotcha!" said Snatcher, the gladiator with the net. He speared the ball with his trident and held it up.

"Give me ball!" said Brutus.

"I want to score," said Snatcher.

Brutus raised his club. "You score always. Goal-hogger. My turn."

Snatcher's face twisted in disgust, but he flung the ball toward the massive, armored gladiator.

Frankie saw his chance as the ball flew through the air. He sprinted to get there first. Brutus saw him coming and swung his club. Frankie dodged before it cracked his skull, and took the ball, leaving Brutus spinning around dizzily.

A few feet away, Max was busy trying to tug the net off of Louise. Charlie was making his way toward their goal, just in case he had to make a save. *It's up to me*, thought Frankie.

Brutus now raised the club and charged like a bull. "Me squash boy!"

You're too slow! Frankie thought, *just like the defender at Kennedy Elementary.* But, just then, out of the corner of his eye, he noticed with a shock that Snatcher was approaching from the other direction, stabbing the air with his trident.

Time for a new plan.

Frankie lifted his foot and blasted the ball at Brutus. It struck his leg, making him stumble.

The crowd sucked in a breath as one: "OOOH!"

The ball bounced back to Frankie, and he took aim and fired again. This time, the ball slammed into Brutus's helmet, spinning it around on his head so he couldn't see.

"AAAH!" gasped the spectators.

Brutus had righted himself and was now swinging his club wildly, getting closer still. Frankie booted the ball hard and this time it hit the club, sending it flying out of the gladiator's hand.

The crowd didn't say anything, which surprised Frankie. Then he turned and saw why.

Captain Lasher was in her chariot again. And she was thundering straight toward him.

CHAPTER 5

Captain Lasher twirled her whip over her head, her eyes gleaming with anger. The horse snorted wildly. The ground shook under Frankie's feet.

"Run!" yelled Louise.

But Frankie knew that if he turned and ran, the chariot would catch him easily. He held his ground.

"Crush him like a grape!" cried Snatcher. Frankie saw him hopping up and down gleefully.

Sand sprayed up from under the horse's hooves and from the churning wheels of the chariot.

"Grind his bones!" growled Brutus.

When Frankie was close enough to see the patterns on Captain Lasher's armor, he bent his legs and dove sideways. He felt the hot breath of the horse and a rush of air as the chariot shot past.

Frankie rolled over and found his feet again as he coughed and blinked in a huge cloud of dust. Squinting, he tried desperately to see out of it.

"Did I get him?" Captain Lasher was shouting. "Did I squash the boy?"

"Where's Frankie?" yelled Charlie. "Frankie!"

"I'm here!" called Frankie, glancing around. "Where's the ball?"

"I see it!" barked Max. The little dog dashed into a patch of swirling sand, just as Snatcher rushed in from the other side.

"Grrrr!"

"Ouch!"

"That's mine!"

"Get off me, you little —"

"Foul!"

"That's my leg!"

Max scampered out from the dust cloud, poking the ball with his nose. As the dust settled, Frankie saw Snatcher squirming on the ground, tangled in his own net.

"You fool!" screamed Captain Lasher.

Max dropped the ball between his paws and passed it to Louise. The chariot turned and headed toward her. Louise kicked the ball over the horse and it dropped to Frankie. There was nothing between him and the goal.

Nothing other than seven feet of muscles and armor: Brutus.

"Come, boy!" Brutus said. "You not get past me now." He spread his trunk-like legs and tossed his helmet aside. He was bald on top, and his head looked like a misshapen potato, but even dirtier. He didn't seem to have a neck at all.

Frankie simply dribbled the ball between his legs.

"Nutmegged him!" shouted Charlie.

The goal was wide open in front of Frankie. *Just keep calm*, he thought.

Twenty feet away, he lifted his foot to shoot.

SPLAT!

Something wet hit Frankie's cheek and he stumbled. The ball rolled away.

Frankie felt his face. *Urgh!* It was slimy. Then his eye fell on a rotten apple on the ground.

SQUISH!

A moldy cabbage landed at his feet and the spectators jeered.

"What's going on?" Frankie muttered. As he looked up, half of a loaf of moldy bread sailed through the air toward his head.

A gloved hand batted it away. "Looks like the home crowd is turning against us," said Charlie. "Look out!"

He reached past Frankie's face and caught a mushy carrot. Now things began to rain down from every side: rotten fruit and vegetables; stinky fish heads; sandals; even a pottery flask that smashed into shards, showering their legs with sharp bits. Frankie skipped from side to side, ducking and jumping, while Charlie did his best to stop as many missiles as possible. But there were too many, even for him, and soon the whole goal was filled with garbage and old food.

Frankie and Charlie backed off toward the center of the field, leaving the ball. Only Max braved the

downpour, to snatch up what looked like a large bone.

A piercing whistle cut through the crowd's boos and all eyes went to the Ref. Frankie saw that the sand in the hourglass timer had run out.

The Ref whispered to the announcer, who then rose to face

the arena. "Friends, Romans, boys and girls!" he proclaimed. "Listen up! Normal time has ended, and the Ref is getting tired. The game will be decided by sudden death. The next team to score will be the victor."

"I wonder what happens to the losers," said Charlie.

"You'll be back in the dungeon for a long time," said Captain Lasher.

"But we've got school on Monday," said Louise. "I've been studying for a math test."

"Well, you can count the rats down there," Captain Lasher replied.

*   *   *

As Frankie's teammates lined up alongside him, servants cleared away the garbage from the goal area. Brutus dragged Snatcher to his feet and they took their places behind their leader's chariot.

Frankie realized for the first time that he was afraid. Not of being run over by a chariot, skewered by a trident, or bear-hugged by a giant. Scared of failing his friends.

"I'm sorry I brought us here," he said.

"It's not your fault," said Charlie. "It was Max who jumped into the portal."

Max looked up from his bone, ears drooping. "Don't blame me – I was just trying to get the ball. I'm a dog. I fetch."

"It's no one's fault," said Louise. "And we're *not* going to lose."

"It's not fair," grumbled Snatcher. "They've got one more player than us."

Captain Lasher grinned. "Not for long." She cracked her whip and the ground in front of her chariot opened up.

"A trapdoor!" said Charlie. "Cool!"

The crowd began mumbling a word, but Frankie couldn't hear what it was. As the chant got louder, he realized they were saying "Ferox! Ferox! Ferox!"

From the trapdoor in the arena floor emerged a huge, shaggy head of tawny fur.

"Um . . . not cool," said Louise.

A lion padded into the arena and the crowd went wild.

CHAPTER 6

The lion looked around, and his black eyes settled on Frankie.

"I guess that's Ferox," said Charlie with a gulp.

Opening his mouth, which looked like a red chasm, the lion roared. Frankie saw gleaming white canine teeth as long as his fingers. *Slingshots, whips, hooves, nets, clubs, and tridents*, thought Frankie. *And now teeth and claws. Can this match get any tougher?*

The whistle blew.

Ferox prowled forward and stood over the ball.

"Anyone want to try tackling him?" asked Frankie hopefully.

Louise and Charlie shook their heads.

Ferox began to walk slowly toward their goal, with the ball under his paws.

We need a distraction, thought Frankie. He turned to Max. "Better give me that bone, Max," he said.

"No way!" said the dog. "It's mine. Finders keepers!"

"If you don't hand it over," said Louise, "it might be all you have to eat for a long time. I don't think the catering in the dungeons is five-star."

Max grumbled, but tossed the bone to Frankie.

Frankie picked it up. "Hey, Ferox!" he called, holding the bone aloft. The lion turned his head and sniffed. "I've got a treat for you!"

Ferox left the ball and ran toward Frankie, who hurled the bone back over his head and watched the lion sprint after it.

Brutus reached the ball at the same moment as Louise. She bounced off the mountain of muscle and landed on her backside.

"Pass it!" called Snatcher.

Brutus set off toward the goal in lumbering strides.

"To me! To me!" shrieked Captain Lasher.

Brutus didn't even look up from the ball.

He wants the glory for himself, thought Frankie. *We'll see about that.*

"Charlie, get out on the wing," he said, dashing after Brutus. "Hey, big guy!" he shouted.

Brutus looked up, grimaced, and swung his club. Frankie dropped into a slide, skidded beneath the club, and managed to get his foot to the ball. He looked for Charlie and saw him moving toward the goal. Frankie passed the ball and watched it fly straight to his friend.

"Great pass!" yelled Louise. "Shoot, Charlie!"

Charlie managed to control the ball. He slammed it toward the goal.

Frankie raised his arms to cheer. . . .

SMACK!

The ball stopped dead as three

metal prongs stabbed it into the ground.

"It's not over yet!" Snatcher cried. As Charlie chased after the ball, the gladiator swished his net across the ground, flicking sand into Charlie's face.

"Hey!" Charlie said. "I can't see!" He staggered back and forth, trying to wipe the sand out of his eyes.

"Take your gloves off!" shouted Louise.

She might as well tell Max to take off his fur, thought Frankie, turning as he heard pounding hooves and rattling wheels.

Captain Lasher was heading for the ball, and Charlie stood right in her path, stumbling blindly. Frankie started running toward his friend.

"Move left!" yelled Louise.

Charlie sidestepped.

"No, my left!" she cried. "Your right."

Charlie went the other way.

Captain Lasher was closing in on him. "He's mine!" she said.

Snatcher was twirling his net, ready to throw it over Charlie's head. "No, he's mine!"

A plan came to Frankie's mind. "Stand your ground, Charlie. Get ready!" He put on an extra burst of speed.

"I'm ... I'm always ready!" said his friend.

Frankie reached Charlie a split second before the chariot. Snatcher's net fell like a shadow overhead. Frankie slammed into his friend, knocking him out of the way.

"Move it!" screamed Captain Lasher.

"Stop!" yelped Snatcher.

Frankie and Charlie landed in a heap. Looking back, Frankie saw Snatcher being dragged along behind the chariot, his net tangled in its wheels. Captain Lasher was hanging on to her reins as the horse galloped around the arena.

"Fools!" roared Brutus. "You let th — ARGH!" He didn't finish his sentence as he was sent spinning by the chariot as it charged past him.

Louise tugged the trident free of the ball. "Let's finish this," she said.

But as they turned toward the goal, something very big, very hairy, and very fierce filled the space between them and the goalposts. It ran its tongue down one of its tusklike teeth. "You forgot about me, didn't you?" Ferox said.

Charlie, finally able to see again,

joined Frankie and Louise. "Any more bright ideas? I don't want to dribble the ball around those claws."

Frankie was about to volunteer when Max trotted up and nosed the ball. "Well, if none of you are brave enough . . ."

As Max the dog walked toward the goal, Ferox the lion strode out to meet him.

"I don't want to look," said Charlie.

When they were a couple of feet apart, Ferox roared, blasting Max's fur like a hurricane.

Max sat back on his haunches, his front paws tucked under the ball.

Frankie began to understand what he was up to — they'd practiced this trick in his backyard last Sunday.

"Aren't you scared?" asked Ferox.

"Why would I be scared?" Max growled.

"Because I'm a lion," said Ferox.

"And you're a puny little dog. I wouldn't even have to chew."

Frankie saw Max quiver and edge forward.

"I know that," said Max. "But the thing is . . ."

"Yes?" growled Ferox, drool spilling from his lips.

"The thing is," said Max, "I'm just causing a distraction."

Max suddenly sprang up, flicking the ball high in the air. Ferox jerked his body to follow its arcing path . . . right to Frankie, who lifted his right foot, twisted his hips, and connected perfectly.

The ball flew between the posts.

CHAPTER 7

Frankie's teammates piled on top of him.

"SUPERGOOAAALL!" shouted Louise.

"Even *I* would have struggled to stop that," admitted Charlie.

"Yeah, not bad," said Max. "I'd lick your face, but it looks sort of dirty."

Frankie patted his head. "You're the most valuable player," he said. "The way you stood up to that lion was incredible."

Max lifted his shoulders in a doggy shrug. "It was nothing. Like Louise said, 'Just a pussycat.'"

Frankie realized that the crowd had gone completely silent. He let his eyes sweep over the thousands of unsmiling faces. *They weren't expecting us to win. . . .*

"Ouch! Ow! No!"

On the other side of the arena, Captain Lasher was giving Brutus and Snatcher a taste of her whip.

"You're pathetic!" she raged. "I'd be better off substituting you for statues, for all the good you did. Call that footwork, Brutus? Call that defense, Snatcher?"

Charlie grabbed the ball out of the goal and held it aloft for the Ref to see.

"The game's over!" he cried. "Now, let us go."

The Ref looked at them, his eyes fierce, but it was the announcer who spoke, looking down his nose at them.

"The game is not over until the Ref decides," he said. "Thumbs up, you may leave. Thumbs down, it's back in the dungeons to fight another day."

The Referee held out his arms, thumbs pointed sideways.

"Dungeons!" called one of the spectators.

"Feed them to Ferox!" called another.

The Ref's thumbs began to turn downward.

"This isn't right!" said Louise. "We won fair and square."

More people were crying out, "Ferox! Ferox!"

"I don't think the rules are the same here," said Frankie. As the shouts grew louder, his hopes began to fade. "I'm sorry, guys," he said. "I tried —"

"Frankie, listen!" said Charlie, a smile starting to spread over his face.

Frankie stopped talking. Louise was grinning, too, and he realized why. The crowd had stopped shouting the lion's name. They were chanting something else.

"FRAN–*KIE*! FRAN–*KIE*! FRAN–*KIE*!"

Frankie glanced at the Ref. His thumbs turned upward and cheers shook the arena. Pride swelled in Frankie's chest.

"Release them!" cried the

announcer. "The winners are Frankie's FC."

Two servants rushed to the main gate and drew back its heavy bolts.

As the doors opened, an incredible sight met their eyes. Frankie saw gleaming temples covered in colorful stone, soaring arches, and tall columns.

Hills covered in grand villas rose in the distance.

"Ancient Rome!" gasped Louise.

"Stop that lion!" bellowed the announcer.

Before the servants could move, Ferox had slipped through the open gates.

"At least one of their teammates escaped the dungeon," said Charlie.

"Let's go home," said Max, scampering ahead.

Frankie followed him, waving to the crowd. But doubts were growing in the back of his mind. What if they couldn't get home?

"Where'd Max go?" asked Charlie, slightly ahead. "He was here a moment ago."

Then Charlie vanished, too.

As Frankie stepped through the gates, sunlight blinded him. When he opened his eyes, he was standing ankle-deep in the sandbox, back in the park.

Clouds hung in the sky and water dripped from the trees. The others hopped out of the wet sand.

"Hey, where've you been?" It was Kevin's voice.

Max barked and Frankie spun around. His brother was walking

toward them, his ball in his hand and his friends following behind.

"We ... we were just playing soccer," said Frankie.

"In a sandbox?" said Kevin, frowning.

"Yes!" said Charlie and Louise together.

Kevin narrowed his eyes suspiciously. "Well, anyway, listen. We thought we'd play a game with you, now that the rain's stopped."

"A game?" said Frankie.

Kevin waved his ball. "Y'know, *soccer*, Frankenstein. Unless you're scared?"

Frankie grinned and looked at the

others. "Scared? No, we don't scare very easily."

As Kevin led them back to the field, he looked Frankie up and down. "Why aren't you soaked? It was pouring a minute ago."

"Um . . ." Frankie searched for an answer.

"We hid under . . . um, the slide," said Louise.

At the dinner table that evening, Kevin was sulking.

"What's wrong with you?" asked Frankie's mom. "Your face looks like you just sucked on a lemon."

"Nothing," grumbled Kevin.

He lost three—one to a group of kids, thought Frankie, finishing his meal. They'd had his favorite dinner: pizza. Max was sitting beside his chair, looking up hopefully for scraps.

Frankie's dad came in with a cup of tea and sat down. "Well, here's something to cheer you up," he said. "I just heard on the radio that there's a lion on the loose in town." He chuckled, obviously not taking it seriously.

Frankie felt blood rushing to his face. *It can't be . . .*

"That's crazy," said Kevin, pushing pieces of crust around his plate.

His dad took a sip from his mug. "Apparently they had to get the zookeeper to track it down," he said. "It's a big guy, with a huge mane."

Frankie managed to recover, and glanced down at Max. "It's probably just a big pussycat," he said with a grin.

ACKNOWLEDGMENTS

Many thanks to everyone at Little, Brown Book Group UK; Neil Blair, Zoe King, Daniel Teweles, and all at The Blair Partnership; Mike Jackson for bringing my characters to life; special thanks to Michael Ford for all his wisdom and patience; and to Steve Kutner for being a great friend and for all his help and guidance not just with this book but with everything.

Help Frankie and his friends through the maze to find their magic soccer ball!

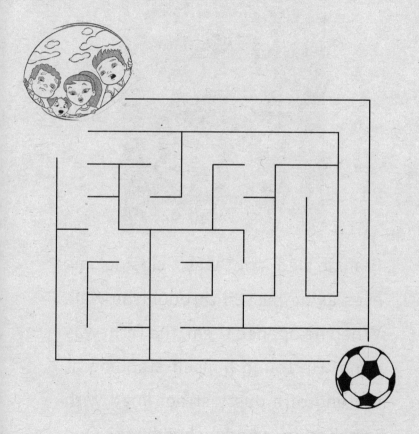

FOLLOW FRANKIE'S ADVENTURES
IN THE NEXT BOOK:

Frankie led the way, closing his eyes as he passed through the wall. When he opened them, the farm was gone. He found himself standing at the end of a dusty street lined with ramshackle wooden buildings. One had a "General Store" sign above the door. Another looked like a saloon, with a wooden porch and swing doors. Shutters covered most of the windows. Beyond the street stretched miles of sandy desert dotted with cacti, and in the distance mountains rose in a haze of heat. What looked like a single line of railroad track vanished into the distance. The magic soccer ball was resting alongside a water trough outside a blacksmith's stall.

Frankie sniffed — the air smelled strangely sweet, like caramel.

"Where *are* we?" asked Charlie. Instead of his school uniform, he was now wearing faded jeans and shirt with a neckerchief and a wide-brimmed hat.

"*When* are we?" asked Louise, who was tugging at the hem of a frilly red dress. "This is not my style at all!"

Frankie glanced down at his own clothes. He saw boots with spurs, pants with leather chaps and a brown shirt. Stitched onto the shirt was his FFC logo.

We must be here to play a game!

Max scampered along, sniffing the ground. "Looks like the Wild West to me!" he barked.